DON'T TOUCH!

Suzy Kline pictures by Dora Leder

PUFFIN BOOKS

PUFFIN BOOKS
Published by the Penguin Group
Viking Penguin Inc., 40 West 23rd Street, New York, New York 10010, U.S.A.
Penguin Books Ltd, 27 Wrights Lane, London W8 5TZ England
Penguin Books Australia Ltd, Ringwood, Victoria, Australia
Penguin Books Canada Ltd, 2801 John Street, Markham, Ontario, Canada L3R 1B4
Penguin Books (N.Z.) Ltd, 182–190 Wairau Road, Auckland 10, New Zealand

Penguin Books Ltd, Registered Offices: Harmondsworth, Middlesex, England

First published in the United States of America by Albert Whitman & Company, 1985
Published in Puffin Books 1988

Lib

Summar uch!"
Dan finds somethin heart's content.
[1. I
87-3288

., Hong Kong
Print a Printing Company

ROYALS
MARK GUB

To Mother with Love S.K.
For my new friend, Billy Lezzer, Jr. D.L.

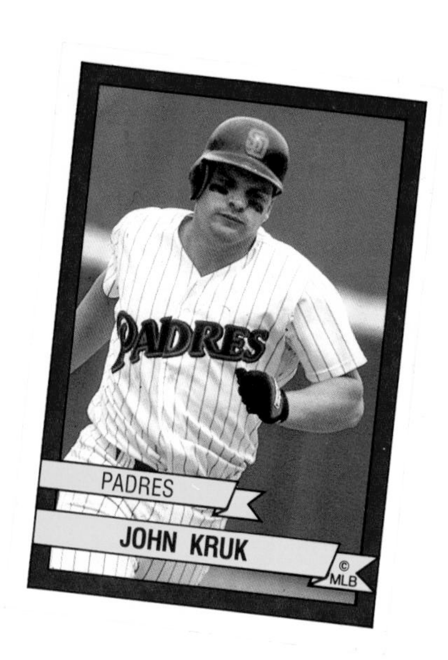
PADRES
PADRES
JOHN KRUK
© MLB

DON'T TOUCH!" says Dad. "That pot is hot!"

“DON’T TOUCH!” says Mom. “That paint is wet!”

"DON'T TOUCH!" says Kate. "You'll crush my rose!"

"DON'T TOUCH!" says the teacher. "Don't touch my desk!"

“DON’T TOUCH!” says the clerk. “Those toys can break!”

"DON'T TOUCH!" says Auntie. "My tools are sharp!"

"DON'T TOUCH!" says Uncle. "My pie's for dinner!"

“DON’T TOUCH!” says Grandpa. “My tackle box is neat!”

"DON'T TOUCH!" says Grandma. "Your scab is healing."

“DON’T TOUCH!” says my sister. “Those tapes are new!”

"DON'T TOUCH!" says my brother. "You'll wreck my hair!"

So . . . I DON'T TOUCH anything!
I go down to the basement . . .

take out my clay and I . . .

SQUISH and SQUEEZE

and SQUASH and SMASH!

PINCH and PUNCH

and POUND and MASH!

TWIST and TWIRL
and STRETCH and STRING!

BLUE
RED
Clay

FLIP and FLOP

and FLING and ZING!

ROLL and SMOOTH

and CRINKLE AND CRUMPLE!
SLAP! SLAP! SLAP! and

WRINKLE and RUMPLE!

POKE!

POKE!

POKE!

POKE!

Then I put the clay away
neatly in each can.

And make a sign for all to read—

DON'T TOUCH!
from
DAN